Bobby *the* BROWN LONG-EARED BAT

Written by
A.S. Mills

Illustrated by
Kate Wyatt

*For my dear family and friends who
have always been so supportive, and
for those bat workers who work so
tirelessly during the bat survey season!*

Foreword
by Chris Packham

Bats are brilliant animals. Birds and insects fly, but the only mammals that truly fly are bats. And then they 'see' with sound! See with sound! That is amazing. It was amazing when I was a kid and it is still amazing now that I'm an old bloke.

Long-eared Bats have always been my favourites because they have big, actually massive, ears. And when I was young I thought they looked 'cute', as opposed to Barbastelle Bats which I thought were 'ugly'. But now I know that in nature there is no 'cute' or 'ugly', there is just effectiveness. And all bats are very effective, superb predators and thus very important in making the world go round. It may sound silly but you and I can't do without bats. Sadly, many bat species are in trouble. Big trouble. We are using too many chemicals in the countryside and we are destroying too many of their homes. Bats need our help. Your help. Now.

Please enjoy this book and then think of a way you can help these amazing animals...

It was June 21st and it was ▮▮▮▮ pecial day, for not only was it midsummer's day, but also Bobby the Brown long-eared bat was born.

In the old farmhouse, a number of mother bats were resting, huddled together with their pups, hanging downwards along the ridge beam in the attic, with their long ears curled backwards like rams' horns. Amongst them were Bobby and his mum.

What a strange world! thought Bobby, who was suddenly upside down and surrounded by lots of noise and batty chatter in the maternity roost; yet Bobby felt safe with his mum, aunts and cousins, for the attic was warm and snug.

Dusk was approaching, and Bobby's mum was thinking of going out to find food. Some of the other mums were taking their new-born pups with them, and the pups clung to their mums tightly as they swooped out of the roost. Bobby's mum, however, decided to leave Bobby in the care of his aunts, in the comfort of the attic, while she went out foraging.

Sometime after sunset, when it was quite dark, Bobby's mum flew out of the roost, making sure that she could not be seen by the inquisitive eyes of the owls that lived nearby. She flew around the trees, catching lots of insects, and after perching in the old barn to feed, she headed off in the direction of her favourite foraging area - the woodland over the hill.

In the roost, Bobby waited patiently. About an hour before sunrise Bobby's mum returned. This happened every night whilst the weather was warm and calm, and Bobby grew and grew over the next few weeks, but how he wished he could go outside too! He would watch some of the older pups bravely venture out during this time.

How exciting! thought Bobby wistfully, but he knew that he would soon be ready to emerge and try his wings outside for the first time, because he practised flying every day with guidance from his mother. Bobby would fly up and down the attic whilst the resident attic mice looked on in awe. "Oh! If only we could have wings!" they sighed.

Ooops! Bobby suddenly found himself on the floor.
He picked himself up and was just about to start flying
again when he spied a small hole in the floorboards. Being
a curious bat, he crawled towards it despite a worried
warning call from his mother. As Bobby approached
the hole, hot air rushed up to greet him. What could be
below? he thought. The warm air was just too enticing so
he decided to crawl further, when suddenly, Whoosh!
He fell and landed on a wooden beam!

Bobby found himself in a cosy farmhouse kitchen with a large fireplace and flagstone flooring. He basked in the heat but the light was a little bit too bright for his liking. He could see the farmer and his wife in two big armchairs by the fireplace, whilst Barney, the collie dog, rested on a rug at their feet. Mollie, the farmyard cat, was busy lapping up milk.

Bobby was unsure what to do next. He couldn't go back to the attic as slippery white paint on the ceiling made it too difficult for him to crawl upwards, so he decided to fly up and down the room, looking for a way out.

Farmer and Mrs Trevelyan were suddenly startled to see this unexpected visitor swooping above their heads. Farmer Trevelyan jumped to his feet.

"What do we have here?" he asked in a kind manner.

Meanwhile Mollie arched her back and leapt high onto the kitchen table to try to catch Bobby, whilst Barney pricked up his ears at all the commotion. Quick-thinking Farmer Trevelyan walked across to the large farmhouse door and opened it, and a gush of cool air entered. After circling the kitchen a few more times, Bobby made his escape through the open door and out into the night. Phew! That was close! he thought.

For the first time in his life Bobby was outside the familiar farmhouse attic. His instincts told him to look for cover, and Bobby found this in an old oak tree, lush and full of leaves, its branches casting shadows on the moonlit floor. The old oak had given shelter to many creatures over the years, and it was Bobby's turn tonight.

An owl hooted in the distance and Bobby waited and watched. Night-time creatures passed below, unaware of Bobby high up in the tree. Time went by. Bobby could see the outline of the farmhouse but he needed to get a clearer view of his surroundings, so he began to echolocate: He flew around the old oak, squeaking his high-pitched batty squeaks, too high for a human ear to hear, and the return echoes helped him create a picture of the area. What a clever bat! Not only did Bobby now have a better view, but his mum and all the bats in the farmhouse roost could hear him calling out too!

Bobby's mum and all the bats in the attic were so relieved to hear Bobby's cries. They swooped out from beneath the eaves to help him, and encouraged him to leave the old oak and join them. Bobby felt confident with the support of his mum and the bats from the roost and he danced happily with them in the night sky.

This was Bobby's first opportunity to go foraging under his mum's expert teaching. Over the hill they flew, along the treeline towards the woodland; the sheep and cows were unaware of their batty friends fluttering noiselessly above, barely detectable flitting shadows against the night sky.

Bobby and his mum hovered and swooped with stealth, and caught lots of insects amongst the woodland trees and the foliage of the hedgerows along the edges of dew-covered fields. They were so busy they almost forgot the time until Bobby's mum called out to remind everyone that the sun would soon be rising, and they should all return home.

Oh, the safety of the farmhouse was a welcoming sight for Bobby, but what an adventure he'd had! In the bats swooped, one by one. Farmer and Mrs Trevelyan were unaware of the bats' busy night.

The day began to break, the birds began to sing, and as the farmer started his working day, the bats snoozed happily in the attic, waiting for the night to come again.

A few Brown long-eared bat facts - courtesy of the Bat Conservation Trust:

- Scientific name *Plecotus auritus*

- Baby bats are called pups

- Mating takes place in the autumn and maternity roosts are formed in late spring with pups taking 60 to 70 days to be born. Most pups are born by mid-July

- Pups grow quickly and are ready to fly outside and are weaned at the age of 6 weeks

- Mums usually have just one pup a year

- Summer roosts can be found in older buildings, barns, churches and trees and usually contain a small number of around 20 to sometimes 50 bats

- Some people are putting up bat boxes to help bats find new homes

- Some Brown long-eared bats may live for up to 30 years though their numbers have declined in Britain due to changing land use, exposure to pesticides and timber treatment, and the loss of suitable feeding and roosting habitats due to more intensive agricultural practices and conversion of barns

- Their long ears enable them to hear very well and they are known as 'whispering bats' because their echolocation frequency is quite quiet

- Their sight and hearing allow them to find food and they may even hear an insect move on a leaf. When foraging, they catch insects in flight and glean insects off foliage leaves and bark

- Their favourite prey is moths, beetles, flies, earwigs and spiders. Prey is eaten in flight but larger insects are taken to a perch in a barn or porch where insects remains such as the wings of moths may sometimes be seen on the floor, indicating that this may be a regular perch for a Brown long-eared bat

- Their broad wings and tail allow slow, highly manoeuvrable hovering flight and steep dives and short glides

- The Brown long-eared bat is found in the UK, Ireland and the Isle of Man but it is absent from Orkney and Shetland and other exposed islands

For further information about bats, please refer to your local bat group and/or the Bat Conservation Trust: http://www.bats.org.uk

A bit about the author:

Angela left a career in banking to study Biology as a mature student at the University of Southampton, and graduated in 2009. Since then, she has worked on many administrative and ecological projects, and works freelance as a licenced bat ecologist, which is how and where the idea for this Bobby story developed. She hopes Bobby's story will educate and inspire both children and adults to learn more about these incredible yet misunderstood creatures. She enjoys volunteering for her local wildlife groups, particularly Dorset Bat Group and East Dorset Bat Rescue and Rehabilitation.

A bit about the illustrator:

Kate grew up in Dorset and went to school in Somerset; during this time, she fell in love with the countryside, although she didn't realise it at the time. Her parents had a great interest in and fascination with all wildlife, and passed their enthusiasm on to Kate. They encouraged her love of drawing and painting, which has made her into one of Britain's best-loved wildlife artists, with her prints selling out of edition within one month of publication.

She firmly believes in the conservation and protection of all Britain's native species and she feels that the most important aspect of her work is to help contribute towards the preservation of British wildlife. She draws from life, sketching and painting outdoors in the countryside.

She was delighted to be asked by Angela to do the illustrations for this book about Bobby and spent many fascinating and enjoyable hours researching this intriguing bat species.